Harvey Moon, Museum Boy
Copyright © 2008 by Pat Cummings
Manufactured in China.

Library of Congress Cataloging-in-Publication Data
Cummings, Pat.
  Harvey Moon, museum boy / written and illustrated by Pat Cummings. —1st ed.
    p.   cm.
  Summary: When Harvey and his pet lizard Zippy go on a school field trip, Zippy gets loose in the museum and they have a harrowing adventure.
  ISBN-10: 0-688-17889-6 (trade bdg.) — ISBN-13: 978-0-688-17889-5 (trade bdg.) 957
  ISBN-10: 0-06-057861-0 (lib. bdg.) — ISBN-13: 978-0-06-057861-9 (lib. bdg.)
  [1. School field trips—Fiction. 2. Lizards—Fiction. 3. Museums—Fiction. 4. Stories in rhyme.]
I. Title.
PZ8.3.C898Ha 2008   2004030056
[E]—dc22   CIP
                                                                              AC

Typography by Jeanne L. Hogle
1 2 3 4 5 6 7 8 9 10
❖
First Edition

To Glenn and Joe,
adventurous boys

WRITTEN AND ILLUSTRATED BY
PAT CUMMINGS

HARVEY MOON, MUSEUM BOY

HarperCollinsPublishers

Tuesday began just like any old day.
But when his mom suddenly said,
"Remember your class has a field trip today,"
A plan popped into Harvey Moon's head.

"Pay close attention to Ms. Yasumi.
Don't fuss. Don't fight. Don't run.
Don't yell. Don't point. Don't *dare* tease the girls."
Harvey groaned as she added, "Have fun."

Once Ms. Yasumi's class reached the museum,
She had them line up, pair by pair.
"Dinosaurs!" "Mummies!" "When do we eat?"
All the yelling gave Zippy a scare.

Now, the lizard was fast, but Harvey was too.
He chased Zippy the moment he ran.
Harvey lost sight of him one or two times,
And then all the screaming began.

Those screams made Zippy run wildly away,
In search of a spot quiet and shady.
Harvey followed. He ran by three people on chairs,
Two guards, and one large fainting lady.

At last he spotted Zippy up under a bush,
So he joined him and said with a grin,
"Let's lie low for a while, but you have to behave.
You jumped out of my bag—now jump in."

It was quiet in the leaves. They both dozed off
Till the museum grew nearly pitch-black.
One little exit sign glowed in the dark.
Zippy peeked out of Harvey's backpack.

In the shadowy room something thudded, then groaned.
"Let's move out," Harvey whispered. "Okay?"
As he inched toward the exit, he heard wings overhead.
"Pterodactyls?" he whispered. "No way!"

He was feeling his way toward the next exit sign,
Past a pyramid made out of plaster.
When a mummy lurched by him, wheezing hot air,
Harvey Moon started walking much faster.

He came upon statues raiding pictures of food,
Swiping cheeses and bread. Then, as one,
Marble cheeks creaked as their marble heads turned.
They spied Harvey. He started to run.

But in the next hall Harvey screeched to a stop,
Smack dab in the midst of a fight.
A Samurai warrior barely missed Zippy's tail
As he swung at a medieval knight.

Harvey leapt on a handy armor-clad horse
And raced toward the daylight ahead.
"Whoa!" called a guard. "How did YOU get in here?"
"I just never got OUT," Harvey said.

To his great surprise, as he left the museum,
He was asked to give live interviews.
His parents weren't mad. Ms. Yasumi seemed glad.
He and Zippy showed up on the news.

Then Hollywood called and wanted his tale
From the moment he left the school bus.
Harvey told the whole truth. "Look, kid," they replied.
"Just leave storytelling to us."

So they made a movie "based on real facts"
With six bad guys and one priceless pearl,
But the guard was the hero, Zippy was a cat,
And Harvey was played by

A GIRL!

Great Buildings

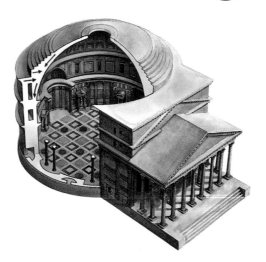

The Nature Company Discoveries Library published by Time-Life Books

Conceived and produced by
Weldon Owen Pty Limited
43 Victoria Street, McMahons Point,
NSW, 2060, Australia
A member of the
Weldon Owen Group of Companies
Sydney • San Francisco • London
Copyright 1996 © US Weldon Owen Inc.
Copyright 1996 © Weldon Owen Pty Limited

THE NATURE COMPANY
Priscilla Wrubel, Ed Strobin, Steve Manning,
Georganne Papac, Tracy Fortini

TIME LIFE BOOKS
Time-Life Books is a division of Time Life Inc.
Time-Life is a trademark of Time Warner Inc.
U.S.A.

Vice President and Publisher: Terry Newell
Editorial Director: Donia A. Steele
Director of New Product Development:
Regina Hall
Director of Sales: Neil Levin
Director of Custom Publishing:
Frances C. Mangan
Director of Financial Operations: J. Brian Birky

WELDON OWEN Pty Limited
Chairman: Kevin Weldon
President: John Owen
Publisher: Sheena Coupe
Managing Editor: Rosemary McDonald
Project Editor: Ann B. Bingaman
Text Editors: Jane Bowring, Claire Craig

Art Director: Sue Burk
Designer: Lyndel Donaldson
Assistant Designer: Regina Safro
Visual Research Coordinator: Jenny Mills
Photo Research: Annette Crueger
Illustrations Research: Peter Barker
Production Consultant: Mick Bagnato
Production Manager: Simone Perryman
Vice President International Sales: Stuart Laurence
Coeditions Director: Derek Barton

Text: Anne Lynch

Illustrators: Kenn Backhaus; Chris Forsey;
Ray Grinaway; Iain McKellar; Peter Mennim;
Darren Pattenden/Garden Studio; Oliver Rennert;
Trevor Ruth; Michael Saunders;
Stephen Seymour/Bernard Thornton Artists, UK;
Roger Stewart/Brihton Illustration;
Rod Westblade; Ann Winterbotham

Library of Congress
Cataloging-in-Publication Data
Lynch, Anne, 1941–
Great buildings / Anne Lynch.
        p. cm. -- (Discoveries Library)
    Includes index.
    ISBN 0-8094-9371-3
    1. Historic buildings--Juvenile literature.
[1. Historic buildings. 2. Architecture--History.]
I. Title. II. Series.
    NA200.L96 1996
    720.9--dc20   95-32821

Manufactured by Mandarin Offset
Printed in China

A Weldon Owen Production